This Book Belongs To

_____

The Wind in the Willows

THE RIVER BANK

Based on the original story by Kenneth Grahame

Retold by Andrea Stacy Leach
Illustrated by Holly Hannon

McClanahan Book Company, Inc.
New York

"Bother!" cried the Mole. He had been working very hard all morning, spring cleaning his little home. He had dust in his throat and eyes, and splashes of paint all over his fur. But spring was moving all around him, calling him to go outside.

So it was no surprise when he flung down his brush onto the floor. "O darn! Hang the spring cleaning!" he said. He headed for the steep little tunnel. "Up we go!" he said, as he scraped and scratched and scrabbled and scrooged, working busily with his little paws.

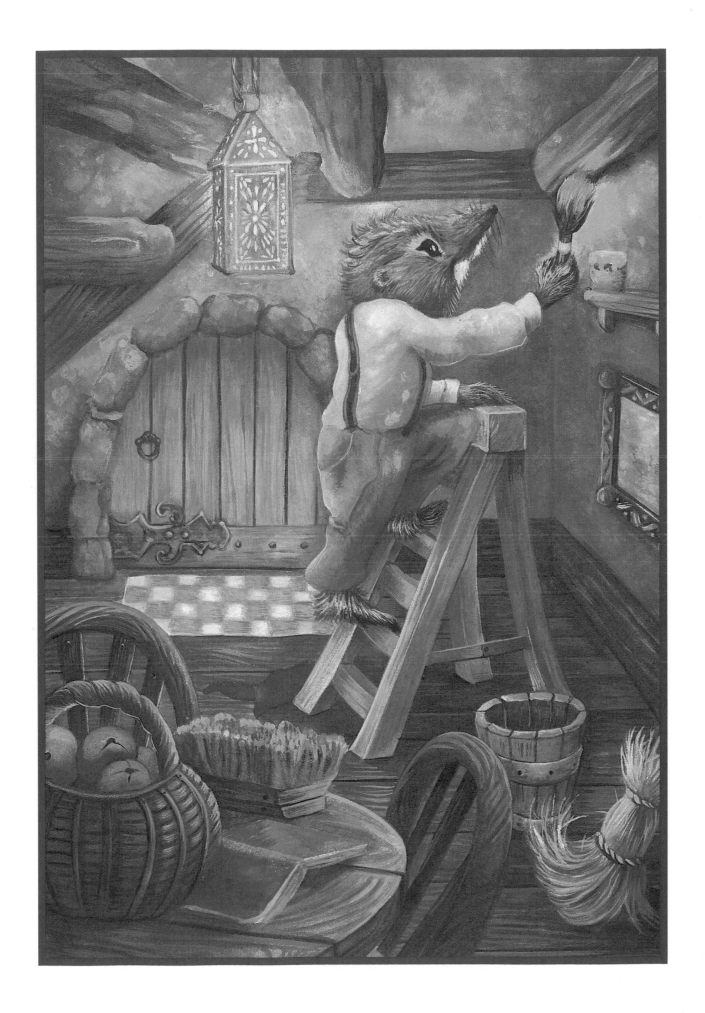

At last, pop! His snout came out into the sunlight, and he found himself rolling in the warm grass of a great meadow.

"This is better than painting," he said. In the delight of spring without its cleaning, he rambled through the meadow until he reached the hedge on the far side. The sunshine warmed his fur

and a gentle wind blew the spring air
about him. "This is fine," he said to himself.
    Suddenly he came to a river. Never in his
life had he seen a river before. All was a-shake
and a-shiver—glints and gleams and sparkles,
rustle and swirl, chatter and bubble. Mole was
fascinated.

In a dark hole in the opposite bank, just above the water's edge, something bright and small twinkled. As Mole gazed at the hole, he saw it wink at him; it was an eye!

A little brown face with whiskers gradually appeared. Small neat ears and thick silky hair topped the face.

It was the Water Rat!

The two animals stood and looked at each other curiously.

"Hello, Mole!" said the Water Rat.

"Hello, Rat!" said the Mole.

"Would you like to come over?" the Rat asked.

"Oh, it's all very well to *talk*," said the Mole. He thought Rat was teasing him, because he did not know how to get to the opposite bank.

But the Rat stepped into a little boat and paddled briskly across the river to Mole. Then he held up his front paw as the Mole carefully stepped down. "Lean on that!" Rat said. "Now then, step lively!" And the Mole, to his surprise and delight, found himself seated in the stern of a real boat.

"This has been a wonderful day!" Mole said. "Do you know, I've never been in a boat before in my whole life."

"What?" cried the Rat, open-mouthed. "What have you been doing? It's the *only* thing," said the Water Rat. "Believe me, my young friend, there is nothing—absolutely nothing—half as much worth doing as messing about in boats."

"Messing about," he went on dreamily, "—about—in—boats—"

"Look ahead, Rat!" cried the Mole suddenly.

It was too late. The boat struck the bank full tilt, and Rat lay at the bottom of the boat.

Rat picked himself up with a laugh. "Look, if you've really nothing else to do, let's go down the river and make a day of it!"

Mole wiggled his toes from sheer happiness. "Let's start at once!"

"Hold on a minute," said the Rat. He tied the boat to a tree and climbed back into his hole. Soon he reappeared with a fat wicker luncheon basket.

"Shove that under your feet," he said to Mole.

The Mole trailed a paw in the water while the Water Rat paddled steadily. "What a jolly life!" said Mole, and the Rat happily agreed.

After a time Rat brought the boat up to the bank and secured it. His friend spread the tablecloth on the grass. "Oh my!" cried the Mole as he opened the packages of food.

They ate and watched Toad rowing badly
down the stream. Rat sighed, "He'll be out of the
boat in a minute if he rolls like that."

When Mole finished packing the luncheon basket, Rat began to paddle home. Mole already felt quite at home in a boat and said, "Ratty! Please, I want to row now!"

The Rat shook his head with a smile. "Not yet, my young friend," he said. "Wait 'til you've had a few lessons. It's not as easy as it looks."

The Mole was quiet for a minute or two. He began to feel jealous of Rat.

Suddenly he jumped up and grabbed the oars. Rat was taken by surprise and fell backwards off his seat.

"Stop it, you silly fool!" cried the Rat.

The Mole made a great dig at the water. He missed the surface altogether. The next moment—Splash!

Over went the boat…and Mole found himself struggling in the river.

O my, how cold the water was! He was sinking. Then Rat's firm paw gripped him by the back of the neck. Laughing, Rat pushed the helpless animal ashore. He rubbed Mole down and wrung some of the wetness out of him. "Now sit in the sun until you're warm and dry, while I dive for the luncheon basket."

When Rat returned, he and the Mole took their places in the boat. "Ratty, I'm sorry. I've been a fool. Will you forgive me?"

"That's all right," Rat said cheerfully. "Look here, I really think you had better stay with me for a little while. I'll teach you to row and swim, and soon you'll be as handy as the rest of us!"

The Mole was so touched by the Rat's kindness he couldn't speak. They went home and had a cheerful supper in front of the fire.

This day was only the first of many like it for
Mole. Each of them was longer and fuller of
interest as the summer progressed. Mole learned
to swim and row, and life on the River was
splendid for him. And with his ear to the reed
stems, he could sometimes catch what the wind
was whispering among them.